My Car by Byron Barton

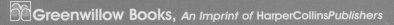 Greenwillow Books, *An Imprint of* HarperCollins*Publishers*

My Car. Copyright © 2001 by Byron Barton. All rights reserved. Manufactured in China. The full-color art was created in Adobe Photoshop™.
The text type is Avant Garde Gothic. Library of Congress Cataloging-in-Publication Data: Barton, Byron. My car / written and illustrated
by Byron Barton. p. cm. "Greenwillow Books." Summary: Sam describes in loving detail his car and how he drives it.
ISBN 978-0-06-239960-1 (pbk.) [1. Automobiles—Fiction.] I. Title. PZ7.B2848 My 2001 [E]—dc21 00-050334
For information address HarperCollins Children's Books, a division of HarperCollins Publishers, 195 Broadway, New York, NY 10007.
First Edition 16 17 18 19 20 SCP 10 9 8 7 6 5 4 3 2 1 Greenwillow Books

I
am
Sam.

This
is
my
car.

I
love
my
car.

I keep my car clean.

My
car
needs
oil

# of gasoline.

My
car
has
many
parts.

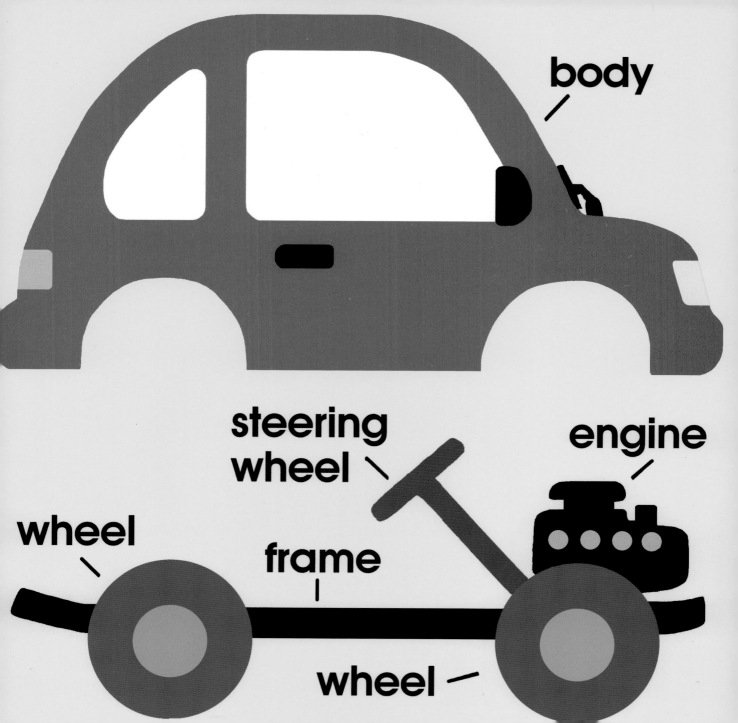

body

steering
wheel

engine

wheel

frame

wheel

My
car
has
lights
to
see
at
night

and windshield wipers

I drive carefully.

I obey

the laws.

for pedestrians.

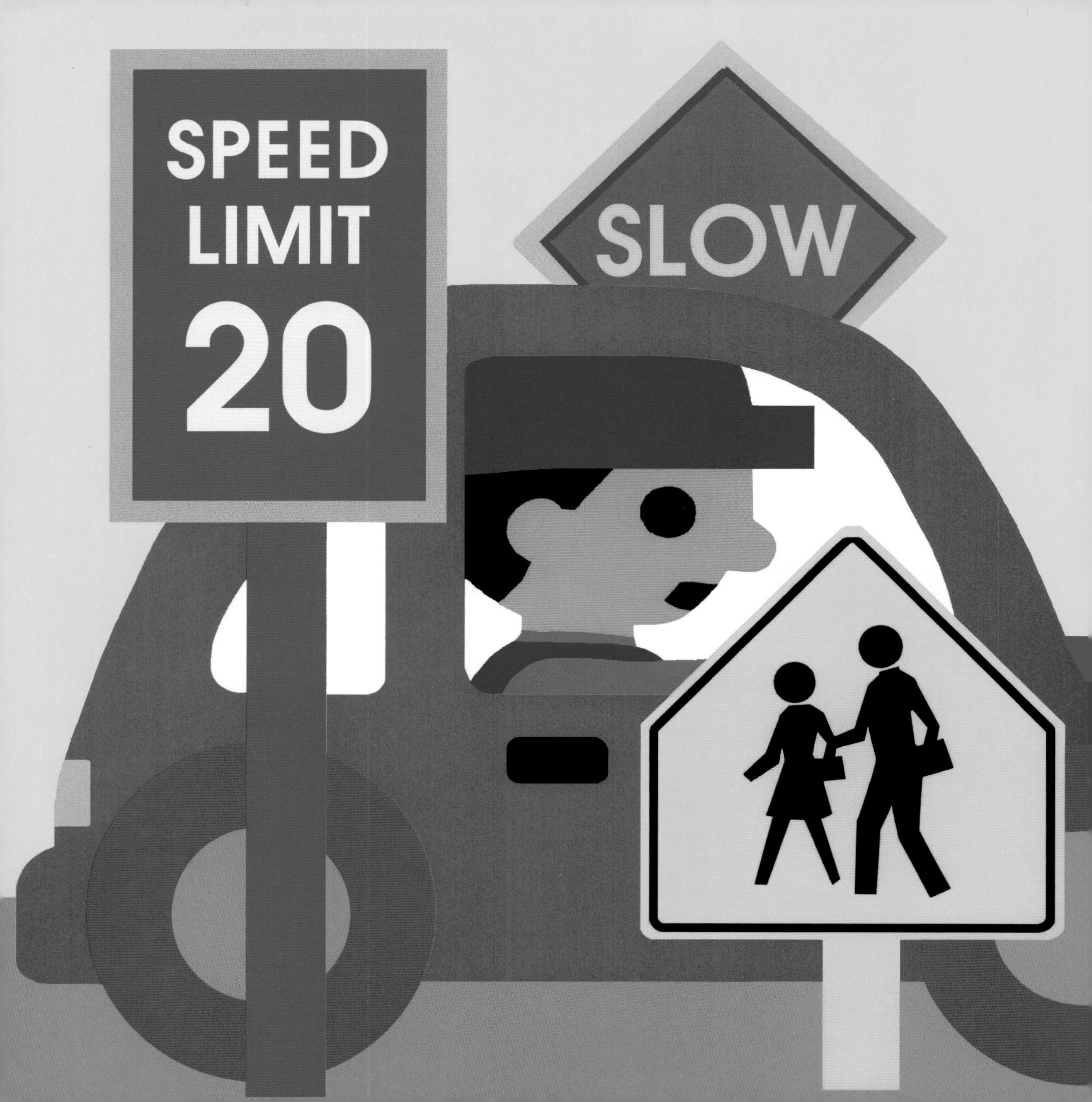
SPEED
LIMIT
20
SLOW

BUS

MAIN ST

ONE WAY

NO
PARKING

I
read
the
signs.

I
drive
my
car
to
many
places.

I drive my car to work.

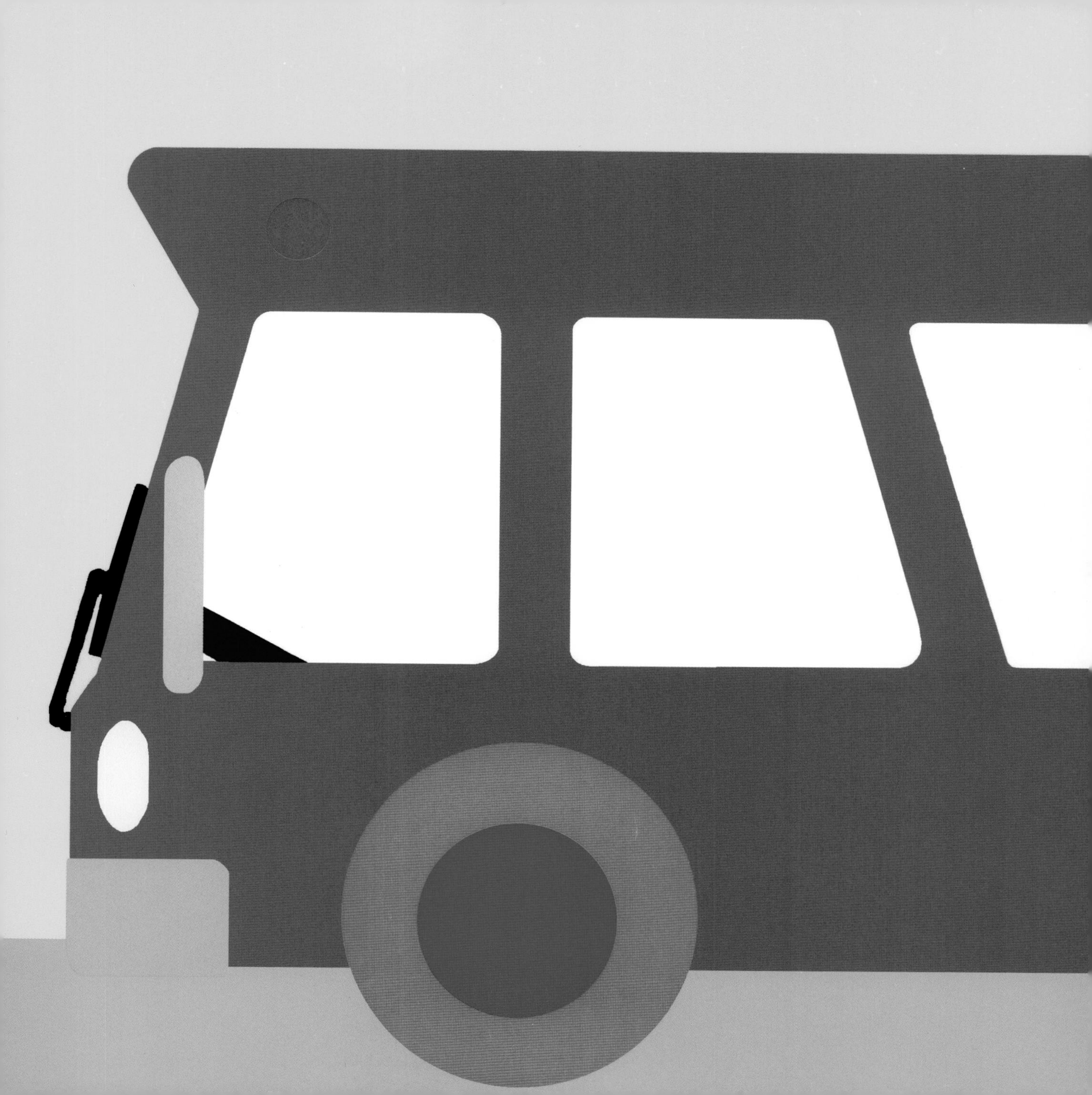

But
when
I work,

BUS

I drive